SCARY GRAPHICS

WHAT'S IN THE WOODS?

STONE ARCH BOOKS
a capstone imprint

Scary Graphics is published by Stone Arch Books,
an imprint of Capstone.
1710 Roe Crest Drive
North Mankato, Minnesota 56003
www.capstonepub.com

Library of Congress Cataloging-in-Publication Data is available on the Library of Congress website.

ISBN: 978-1-4965-9799-1 (library binding)
ISBN: 978-1-4965-9803-5 (ebook PDF)

Summary: It's Andy's first year at camp and the older boys are telling him stories of mysterious faerie circles hidden in the ancient woods. If you disturb a circle, they say, you'll be snatched away forever by vicious creatures. Andy assumes it's all a joke, but when he stumbles into one, he'll find out there may be some truth to the legends after all . . .

Editor: Abby Huff
Designer: Brann Garvey
Production Specialist: Katy LaVigne

Printed and bound in the USA.
PA117

WHAT'S IN THE WOODS?

BY
STEVE FOXE

ILLUSTRATION BY
JUAN CALLE

COLOR BY
LUIS SUAREZ AND
SANTIAGO CALLE
(LIBERUM DONUM STUDIOS)

COVER ART BY
ALAN BROWN

WORD OF WARNING:

SOME CAMPFIRE STORIES ARE JUST MYTHS.
OTHERS ARE REAL—VERY REAL.

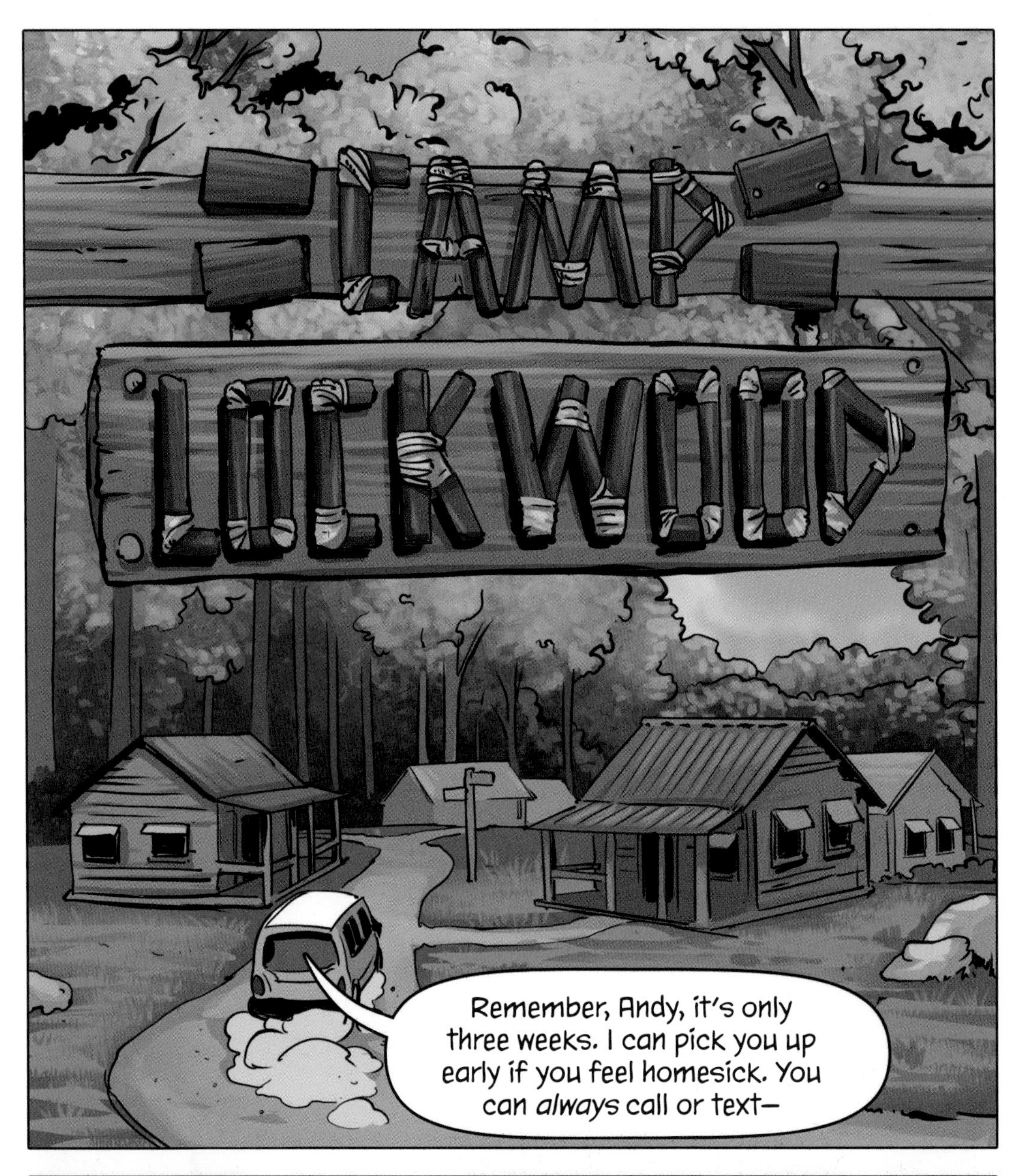
CAMP
LOCKWOOD
Remember, Andy, it's only three weeks. I can pick you up early if you feel homesick. You can *always* call or text—

Mom! *Please!* I can handle it.

I just love you and want you to have a fun, *safe* time. Don't do anything you don't feel comfortable doing.

And don't try too hard to impress the other boys.

Attention, Camp Lockwood campers! Please check in to your assigned cabins.

Really gotta go. Bye, Mom!
Bye, honey! Remember, it's only three weeks! See you soon!

Here goes nothing–
RUSTLE

What?
RUSTLE
RUSTLE
Grrr...

RAWR!
Ahh!

Welcome to Cabin 13, new kid.

Ready to call your mommy yet?

Hey, Andy, right? I'm Fred.
Don't mind Dalton. He likes to give new kids a hard time.
And you're the only first-year in Cabin 13.

But he'll get bored with it in a few days. He always does.
I hope so. There's *no way* I'm putting up with three weeks of bullying.

The next day...
Watch out for lake monsters, new kid.
Mommy isn't around to save you.

Ahh!
SPLASH!

What are you making?
It's a robotic—

CRRASH

Oops. Slipped. My bad, new kid.

Um, I *really* don't like heights...
Everyone who says that ends up loving the ropes course after they give it a try!

You don't understand. I feel sick just looking at it.
Err... Then why don't you head back to the main hall? We can find another activity for you.

That's right, new kid.
Go call *mommy* for a ride home.

That night...
Hey, my stuff!

Oh, sorry, new kid. I thought you'd be on your way back home. Anyway, this is *my* bunk now.
But I'm sure there's room for you in the crawl space under the cabin ... as long as you don't mind spiders.

Get. Off. My. BUNK!
YANK!!

You think you're tough, new kid?

If you don't learn some respect, we'll let the forest deal with you. Tie you up and leave you in a *faerie circle.*
SHOVE

Ha! "Fairy circle"? Is that *supposed* to be scary?
That sounds like something from my little sister's princess birthday party.

Not "fairy" like glitter and tiaras. Old-school *faeries.* The nasty kind.
Yo, Isaac, get the lights.

Legend has it that the woods around Camp Lockwood are home to ... *creatures.*

These creatures have ways of staying hidden.
But they leave faerie circles to mark their territory—and warn humans when we're getting too close.

If you see a weird circle made of rocks, twigs, and bones, and you don't turn and run the other way...
Snrrf!

Well, let's just say we'll have an open bunk after all.

Whatever. You can't scare me with some lame story that's obviously made up.

Hey, I'm just trying to be a responsible cabin captain by warning you. You wouldn't be the first camper we've lost.
But if you don't believe me, go look for yourself ... if you're *brave* enough.

The next morning...
Fred! Wait up a second.

I'm going off to find one of those "faerie circles." I'm going to bring back proof to show Dalton I'm not scared.
Dude, they probably aren't even *real*. You can't take Dalton's teasing so personally.

Forget it. I can do this by myself.
Hey! You could get lost in there!

They all think I'm a scared little chump. I'll show them.

Dalton has probably never had someone call his bluff before.

If I can even find one of these faerie things...

Whoa.

This is it?! It looks like my grandma's flower garden!

Dalton and his goons probably make these to scare the younger campers.
Well, it's not going to work on *this* new kid.

Wow, they really go all out.

Okay, now to get back to the path. Just a few minutes back ... this way? Wait, this looks different.

SCRTTTCH
I swear I *just* came through here.
SCRTTTCH

And I know the clearing was *right* there.
SCRTTTCH

Okay, Andy, breathe.
SCRTTTCH
SCRTTTCH
Dalton is probably playing another trick on you by ... moving the forest?
Ugh, I must've gotten turned around.

SCRTTTCH
SCRTTTCH
And what is that *noise*?!

SCRTTTCH
Ahh!

No!

Let me go!
Let me go!
Calm down.
It's just me!

Where—
how am I back
here?
You've
been gone for
an hour!
The counselors are freaking out.
I came back to where you ran off and
saw you screaming in the bushes.

An hour...?
That doesn't
make any
sense.

Whatever.
I got what I
was looking for.
Let's get back
to the cabin.
I have
something
to show
Dalton.

There you are, new kid. Did you get lost in—
Good try on the faerie circle prank, Dalton. But I called your bluff.

What?! Get this junk off my bed, new kid!

Wait, what is this?

Drop the act, Dalton. I know you made it.

Uh, no. I didn't.
I have never seen this stone before in my life.

If you're trying to out-prank me, nice try.
But get this creepy stuff out of here.

Sure, and that wasn't you and your goons chasing me through the mist earlier?

What are you *talking* about?
We were on the hike the whole time.

And, uh, Andy? There was no mist earlier.
It was super clear this morning.
Great, now you're in on it too, Fred? I thought you were better than them.

Listen, new kid. You're starting to freak everyone out. We didn't plant any faerie circles for you to find.

Sure, I was teasing you earlier.
But the reason we tell the faerie circle story is because a kid really *did* disappear in the woods years ago. He was never found.

I never really believed in all the legends, and I don't know *what* you found, but...

...something about that stone isn't right.
I *don't* want it in the cabin. Take it back to the woods.

So either Dalton is really committed to this prank, or he's a bigger scaredy-cat than he lets on.
SLAM!

No way am I lugging this back.
Not with that rabid squirrel or whatever I saw on the loose.

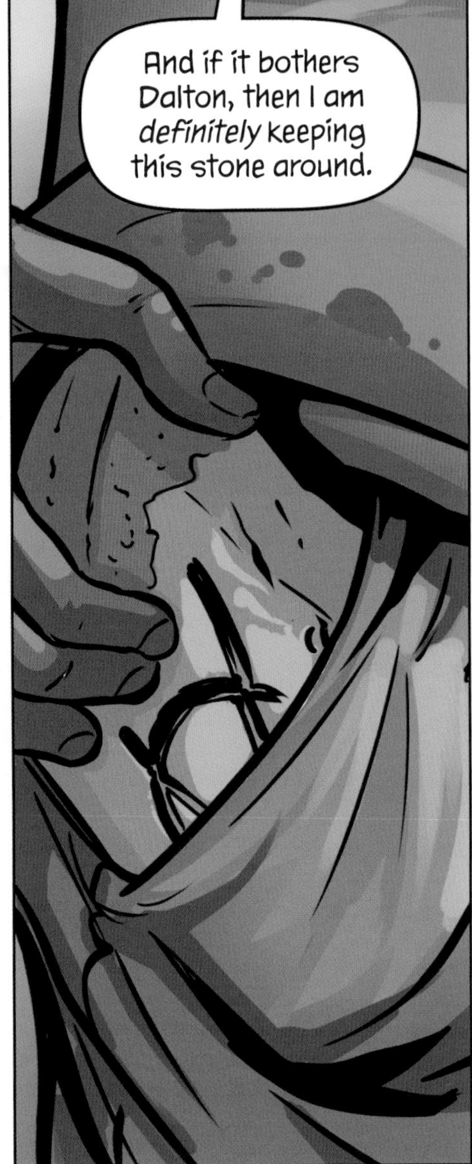
And if it bothers Dalton, then I am *definitely* keeping this stone around.

That night...

THE CIRCLE IS BROKEN...
...RETURN OUR TOKEN.

SCRTTTCH
SCRTTTCH
Huh? That noise...?

GIVE US BACK THE STONE!

Ahh!
FWIIIS

Cut it out, guys! It's the middle of the night. This isn't funny.
CLICK

Cut *what* out? We were all asleep.
No one is bothering you, new kid!

I heard you! You were whispering about the stone I found. Stop trying to scare me!

CLICK
Turn the lights back on! You're freaking us out!
I didn't touch them, I—

THE CIRCLE IS BROKEN!
RETURN OUR TOKEN!
Who was that?!
Forget this! I'm getting out of here.

Come on, Andy! Something bad is going on. We need to get a counselor.
I don't need a counselor! And I don't need any of you.

You can all run! I know this is just some big trick.

I'm not going to let you embarrass me with a silly fairy-tale story.

It's just a trick. It *has* to be.
THE CIRCLE IS BROKEN...
SCRTTTCH
SCRTTTCH
...RETURN OUR TOKEN.

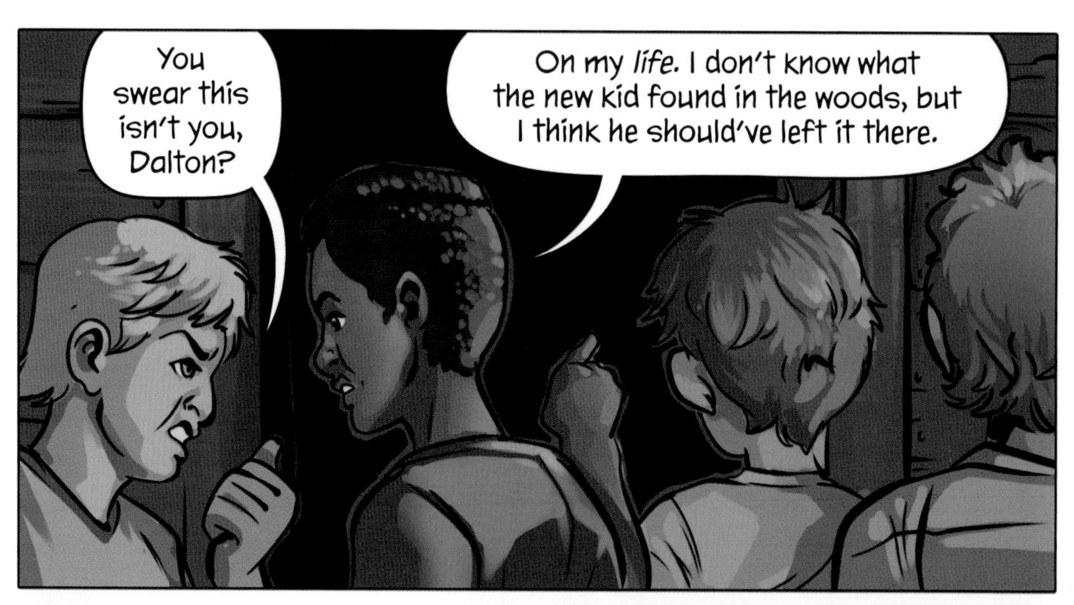
You swear this isn't you, Dalton?
On my *life*. I don't know what the new kid found in the woods, but I think he should've left it there.

Yo, new kid! This isn't a prank! It's not safe in there!
Please come out, Andy! We—

SCRTTTTTTTTTTTTTTTTCH

SCRTTTCH
SCRTTTCH

THE CIRCLE IS COMPLETE!
THE CIRCLE IS COMPLETE!

What's going on? You boys are waking up the entire camp!

Don't go in!
The faeries! The faeries took–
He broke the circle and–
The lights went out and there were red eyes and–

Enough! One at a time. Dalton, what happened?
The new kid– Andy. He took ... *something* from the woods.
Then *they* came to get it back.

They? Who's they? Dalton, you've taken your pranks too far this time.

...Andy?

The End

LOOK CLOSER

1. We can't see Andy's face on this panel from page 11, and he doesn't say anything. But the art still gives clues on how he's feeling. Describe his emotions. What might he be thinking?

2. Do you think Dalton believes in his own story about faeries? Why or why not? Use examples from the art and text to support your answer.

3. A panel that takes up a whole page is called a splash. Why do you think the illustrator decided to use one on page 18? How would the moment be different if the panel was smaller?

4. Whose eyes are glowing in the background? What makes you think that? Can you find the red eyes anywhere else in the story?

5. Andy is nowhere to be seen at the end. What will happen next? Do the faeries come back? Does anyone try to rescue Andy? Will he ever be seen again? Write the story.

THE AUTHOR

Steve Foxe is the author of more than 40 children's books and comics properties including Pokémon, Transformers, Adventure Time, Steven Universe, DC Super Friends, and Grumpy Cat. He lives in Queens, New York, far away from the deep, dark woods and everything hiding inside of them.

THE ILLUSTRATOR

Juan Calle is a former biologist turned science illustrator, trained at the Science Illustration program at California State University, Monterey Bay. Early on in his career, he worked on field guides of plants and animals native to his country of origin, Colombia. Now he owns and works in his art studio, LIBERUM DONUM, creating concept art, storyboards, and his passion: comic books.

bluff (BLUHF)—a lie meant to make yourself appear better or more powerful than you are

committed (kuh-MIH-ted)—going to do something all the way, no matter what

creature (KREE-chur)—a living thing, often a strange one that is not like other animals

embarrass (em-BAR-uhss)—to cause someone to feel silly and uncomfortable in front of others

goon (GOON)—a person who does what someone else says and is often ordered to scare and bully others

impress (im-PRESS)—to make someone think better of you, usually by doing something or acting a certain way

legend (LEH-juhnd)—an old story that's been told many times and by many people but cannot be proven to be true

prank (PRANGK)—a trick that is done to someone as part of a joke

territory (TER-uh-tor-ee)—an area of land on which something lives and protects from others

token (TOH-kuhn)—a thing that has special meaning

warn (WORN)—to tell someone about a bad thing that might happen

SCARY GRAPHICS

NOT SCARED YET? DARE TO READ THEM ALL...

ONLY FROM CAPSTONE